# QUICKREADS

# RUBY'S
# TERRIBLE SECRET

JANET LORIMER

SADDLEBACK
EDUCATIONAL PUBLISHING

# QUICKREADS

SADDLEBACK
EDUCATIONAL PUBLISHING
www.sdlback.com

**Copyright ©2010, 2005 by Saddleback Educational Publishing**
All rights reserved. No part of this book may be reproduced or transmitted in any form or by any means, electronic or mechanical, including photocopying, recording, or by any information storage and retrieval system, without the written permission of the publisher.

ISBN-13: 978-1-61651-218-7
ISBN-10: 1-61651-218-0
eBook: 978-1-60291-940-2

Printed in Guangzhou, China
0611/CA21100814

15 14 13 12 11    2 3 4 5 6

■ ■ ■

*T*his area hasn't changed at all, Melinda thought, as she slowed her car for a turn. *It looks just as it did when I left seven years ago.*

She turned off the highway and onto a narrow road that wound up the mountain. At first Melinda could see houses tucked away behind the trees. But the higher up the mountain she drove, the fewer houses she saw. Then there were no houses, and the road narrowed even more. Before long it was just a rutted dirt path.

At last Melinda spotted her grandmother's farmhouse just ahead. For a moment her breath caught in her throat. She wondered if the old woman would welcome her, or—

Melinda parked under a big oak tree. She climbed out of the car and stretched. *I'm tired and hungry,* she thought. *I sure hope Ruby doesn't send me back down the hill.*

Suddenly the front door opened and Ruby stepped onto the porch. She gazed at her granddaughter as if she couldn't believe her eyes. "Melinda?"

"Ruby!" Melinda ran across the yard and up the wooden steps.

They grabbed each other in a big hug. Then Ruby held Melinda back at arms' length. "Let me look at you," she said. "Oh, Melinda, you're all grown up—and you're so beautiful!"

Melinda smiled. "I've missed you so much, Ruby," she said.

"And I've missed you, too," Ruby whispered, her eyes spilling tears. "Every day for the last seven years."

Melinda's smile disappeared. "You *have*? But you were the one who made me go! I was only 16 when you packed me off to live with Aunt Kay and Uncle Jim. I hardly knew them then—and I didn't want to leave. Why did you send me away?"

Ruby grasped Melinda's arm. "I did it for *you*," she said, nervously pulling Melinda toward the front door. "I thought you'd have better opportunities if you lived in the city. And just what are you doing back here now, child?"

Melinda sighed. "I was in an automobile accident a couple of weeks ago. I'm okay, but the doctor told me to take some time off from work. I decided to come for a visit."

Ruby looked upset. "Oh, Melinda, honey, that was a bad idea," she groaned. "You can't stay here."

"Why not?" Melinda demanded. "What did I do to make you—"

"Oh, no, Melinda!" Ruby exclaimed. "It wasn't anything *you* did, child. It's —it's just the danger! As long as you stay here, you're not safe."

■ ■ ■

Melinda didn't know what to say. Her grandmother's words shocked her. She'd noticed how nervously Ruby had glanced around the yard. And she wondered why Ruby had grabbed her arm and so quickly hustled her into the house.

"I'll fix you something to eat," Ruby said quickly. "Then you have to get back down the mountain, honey. You can stay at that new motel on the highway. Tomorrow—"

"Hold on," Melinda said stubbornly. "I'm not going anywhere. What's this danger you're talking about?"

Ruby took a deep breath. "I'm not saying another word about it. There are some things you don't need to know. Just do what I tell you and—"

"*No!*" Melinda said firmly as she crossed her arms over her chest. "I'm not 16 anymore, Ruby. I'm an adult and I want you to tell me why—" Her voice trailed away as she thought about something. "Does this 'danger' have anything to do with the reason my mother went away?"

Ruby groaned and her eyes filled with tears again. "I didn't think you remembered anything about that."

Melinda frowned. "I don't really remember. I was so young when she left. How old was I?"

"Just a baby," Ruby said.

Melinda followed the old woman into the kitchen. "Are you hungry, child?" Ruby asked.

Melinda nodded, but she wasn't going to let Ruby change the subject that easily. "So if there's danger here, why do *you* stay?"

Ruby glanced at her granddaughter in surprise. "Why, this is my home, Melinda. I can't leave. Besides, there's no danger to *me*—not anymore."

Melinda was puzzled. She wanted to dig deeper into the mystery, but Ruby wouldn't let her. "You go on and wash up now, honey," Ruby said. "Then we'll have our dinner."

■ ■ ■

They talked over dinner. Ruby asked a lot of questions about her granddaughter's job in the city. But each time Melinda tried to ask her anything about the danger, the old woman changed the subject.

Their talk brought back memories of Melinda's childhood. "Ruby, did you give away that stuffed teddy bear I used to have?" Melinda asked.

Ruby laughed. "Oh, no. I knew he was your favorite. I figured that I'd send him to you someday."

Ruby led Melinda upstairs to her old bedroom. Everything there had been kept exactly as Melinda had left it so long ago.

Ruby opened a battered wooden chest at the foot of the bed. Melinda's favorite toys were still packed inside, along with special childhood clothes and a few books.

Melinda dropped to the rag rug on the floor and began to pull things out of the chest. Before long she realized it was getting dark.

She glanced up at Ruby, who was sitting on the bed. The old woman was watching her with eyes filled with love.

"Ruby, please let me stay with you," Melinda said. "I swear I'll be good. I'll do whatever you tell me."

Ruby sighed. Then she nodded. "I don't have the heart to send you away again," Ruby said, her voice breaking. "I've missed you so much, Melinda. But you have to promise me that you won't go into the forest. Not even during the day."

Melinda frowned. "Okay, I promise. Although I don't know why—"

"It doesn't matter why," Ruby said crossly. "Just *don't!*" She stood up and headed for the door. "I'm going downstairs to clean up the kitchen now. Don't stay up too late, honey."

■ ■ ■

As soon as Ruby left the room, Melinda began searching through the trunk again. She found her first doll, several broken crayons, and a handful of old photos that were taken at a childhood birthday party.

*I remember that party,* Melinda thought. *That's me and there's Ruby. And there's*— She frowned, trying to remember the name of the other little girl in the photo. Then it came back to her: Ariana.

*I'd forgotten all about Ariana,* Melinda thought to herself. *I wonder whatever happened to her?*

Melinda hurried downstairs. She found Ruby drying the dishes.

"Ruby, do you remember Ariana?" Melinda asked. "She was the little—"

The dish slipped from Ruby's hands and smashed on the kitchen floor.

"Oh, look out!" Melinda exclaimed. "Don't cut yourself. I'll get the broom."

Then she caught sight of Ruby's face. It had turned as white as the dishtowel she was holding!

"Sit down now, Ruby," Melinda whispered. "What's wrong?"

"N-nothing," the old woman stammered. "I guess I'm just kind of clumsy tonight."

Melinda cleaned up the broken china and finished drying the dishes. Ruby sat at the table and watched. Melinda could tell that her grandmother was still badly shaken.

"I'm sorry about the dish," Melinda said. "Was it one of your favorites?"

"Oh, no," Ruby said with a shaky laugh. "It was just a cheap old thing I got at a secondhand store."

"About Ariana—" Melinda started to say. She watched as again the color quickly disappeared from Ruby's face.

"I don't know what happened to her," Ruby said sharply. "And I don't care. I hope I never see her—" She stopped, embarrassed at her outburst. "I-I mean—" Her voice trailed away. "I don't know what I mean," Ruby said at last. "I'm just tired, and I'm not making sense. It's time for me to go to bed, Melinda. You should, too."

"I will," Melinda said slowly. "You go on ahead, Ruby. I'll be up soon."

■ ■ ■

After Ruby went upstairs, Melinda wandered into the parlor. She sat in Ruby's old rocking chair and rocked. The chair still made the same comforting squeak. Melinda smiled.

Then she remembered how shaken Ruby had been when Ariana's name was mentioned. How strange! Did Melinda's childhood playmate have something to do with the danger?

Melinda thought back to the day she'd first met Ariana. That morning, she'd been picking wild blackberries at the edge of the forest.

*I was about 11 years old,* Melinda recalled. *Ariana and I often played in the forest. I wanted her to come to my birthday party. But Ruby got upset when I introduced her to my friend.*

Melinda had never been able to figure out why Ruby disliked Ariana.

*And Ariana would never take me to her*

*house to meet her family. Why not?* Melinda wondered.

The two little girls went on meeting to play in the forest for a couple of years. But by then Melinda was getting tired of their childish games.

*I had outgrown my dolls and my coloring books,* she thought. *I was a teenager—interested in boys and makeup. So I stopped meeting Ariana.*

Something upsetting happened to Ruby when Melinda had turned 16. Whatever it was had made her send Melinda away to live with Aunt Kay and Uncle Jim.

But what was it? Melinda was determined to find out. She yawned. For now, it was time to get some sleep.

As she stood up, she spotted Ruby's old picture album. Melinda smiled. *I remember this. I haven't looked at these old photos in years.*

She tucked it under her arm and headed for her old bedroom.

■ ■ ■

Melinda sat up in bed with the album on her lap. Several of the first photos she saw were of Ruby as a little girl. Melinda decided she'd look at those later. Right now, she wanted to find the pictures of her mother.

In the middle of the album were photos of Ruby as a bride and later as a young mother. Melinda's mother, Rose, had been Ruby's youngest child.

Melinda turned the pages of the album slowly. There was a picture of Rose as a baby and one as a young girl playing on an old tire swing. *She must have been about five or six years old then,* Melinda thought fondly.

When she glanced at the next photo, her hand froze and her eyes grew wide with shock. "No! It can't be!" she gasped.

In the photo, Rose was standing next to another little girl—Ariana!

*That can't be Ariana,* Melinda thought. Then a possible explanation came to her. Maybe her mother's playmate had grown up to be Ariana's mother. That would explain the resemblance.

She studied the photo again. *But my mother's friend is wearing the dress Ariana always wore. I remember feeling sorry for her because I thought she had only that one dress.*

Melinda shivered. Obviously, there was no way Ariana could have remained a little girl for 20 years or more!

But just the mention of Ariana's name had unnerved Ruby. What did her grandmother know about the girl?

Suddenly Melinda had a strange feeling. She opened the album to the beginning. As a child, she'd never paid close attention to the details in these old black-and-white pictures. But now she studied each photo carefully.

Melinda found a picture of Ruby as a baby and another of her holding a kitten. And then— Melinda gulped. There was a photo of Ruby with some other boys and girls. Ruby looked about 10 years old. Standing right beside her was—Ariana!

Melinda was wide awake now. This was

way beyond impossible. It was becoming downright scary!

*The camera doesn't lie,* Melinda reminded herself. *Well, there are two possible answers. Maybe these are three different little girls, but they're all about the same age and they're dressed alike. Either that, or this same little girl has remained the same age for more than 60 years. But there's no way on earth such a thing could happen!*

Melinda sighed. "Ruby knows more than she's telling me. Tomorrow, I'm going to get to the bottom of this."

■ ■ ■

When Melinda woke up, the sun was already high in the sky. She dressed quickly. Then, grabbing the album, she hurried downstairs to find her grandmother.

Ruby was frying pancakes. When she heard Melinda's footsteps, she turned to greet her granddaughter with a big smile. Then she saw the photo album, and her happy smile froze on her face.

Melinda held the album out to her grandmother. "I found all the pictures of Ariana," she burst out. "Ruby, what's this all about? How can—"

"Sit down," Ruby said with a sigh. "I'll tell you what I know, Melinda—although I hoped I'd never have to." Ruby sat across the table from Melinda. "You know that I was born on this farm, and that I grew up here. When I was about eight years old, I met a little girl in the forest."

"Ariana?" Melinda asked.

Ruby nodded. "I was the youngest child in my family. I had no playmates my age, so I was happy to have a new friend. Ariana said she didn't have any brothers or sisters. So she was glad to have a new friend, too."

"Did you ever meet her family?" Melinda asked.

Ruby shook her head. "No. For some reason Ariana would never take me to meet them. All she would say was that she and her parents lived up near the top of the mountain. She didn't seem to want to talk about her family at all."

"But she came here to the farm, didn't she?" Melinda said.

"Once or twice," Ruby said. "The second time she came, my father took the picture you saw in the album."

"Then what happened?" Melinda asked, trying to keep the impatience out of her voice.

"We were friends for a long time," Ruby said sadly. "But when I began to change—to grow older—I noticed that Ariana stayed the same. I guess I told myself that some people just mature faster than others.

"I went on to high school," Ruby continued, "and then I met your grandfather. We got married and started a family. I was busy and happy with my life, and I forgot about Ariana. I suppose I figured she'd grown up, too, and her family had moved away."

Melinda was fascinated. "What happened next?" she asked.

"As you know, my youngest child was your mother," Ruby said with a smile. "When Rose was about nine, she came home talking about a little girl she'd met in the forest. I didn't think much about it. A lot of new people were moving to this area then."

"But she brought Ariana home to meet you, didn't she?" Melinda said.

Ruby took a deep breath. "I was shocked at first. Then I told myself that this had to be the *daughter* of the little girl I'd known. It couldn't be the same child."

Melinda nodded. "That's what *I* thought last night when I saw the photo of my mother and Ariana. But when I saw the photo of *you* and Ariana—I didn't know what to think."

"Rose had the same experience that I did," Ruby continued. "After a while, she outgrew Ariana. She married your father and then you were born. The two of you came back here to live after your daddy died in that accident.

"A few years later I heard Rose and Ariana talking in the backyard. Your mother was hanging clothes on the line. You were playing on a blanket where she could keep an eye on you.

"Ariana was angry that Rose wouldn't play with her anymore. She kept saying over and over, 'Why won't you play with me?'"

Melinda felt a cold chill run up her spine. "That must have frightened you," she said.

"Oh, it did," Ruby admitted. "I tried to warn Rose—but I'm afraid she didn't realize the danger. She turned her head toward the clothesline for an instant. When she looked back, Ariana was gone. And so were you!"

■ ■ ■

Melinda gazed at Ruby in shock. "Ruby! Are you saying that Ariana *kidnapped* me?"

Ruby's eyes filled with tears at the terrible memory. "Rose took off after Ariana. But then—" she sobbed.

Melinda sat forward in her chair.

"Rose didn't come back," Ruby whispered. "Instead, Ariana and her parents brought you home."

"But where was my mother?" Melinda burst out.

Ruby's lips tightened. "They told me there'd been an accident. They said Rose had fallen and she wasn't—she wasn't coming home."

Ruby broke down sobbing.

Melinda stared at her grandmother in astonishment. "Why didn't you *do* something?" she demanded. "You should have called the sheriff!"

Ruby shook her head. "I was afraid," she whispered. "Melinda, those people aren't like us. I don't know what they are—but they aren't human. They just *can't* be! They warned me that if I told anyone the truth about Rose, something terrible would happen to *you*!"

Melinda sat back, stunned by what Ruby had told her.

"I told everyone that Rose left home," Ruby went on. "It was an awful lie, but I couldn't tell the truth. What if they came back and took you, too?"

"Ruby, do you think Ariana's family killed my mother?" Melinda asked.

"I-I don't know." The old woman rocked back and forth in her chair, trembling. Melinda knelt by her grandmother's chair and put her arms around her. For so many years Ruby had lived in such fear, holding onto her terrible secret.

"It's okay," Melinda whispered. "You don't have to be afraid anymore. We're going to figure it out, and then—"

At that moment they both heard a child's high voice calling. "Melinda! Come out and play!"

■ ■ ■

The childish words spoken in that high voice made it hard for Melinda to breathe. But her fear quickly turned to anger. Ariana was no longer a mystery; now she was the enemy.

Melinda ran out to the porch. Looking exactly as she had seven years ago, Ariana stood on the front path. Her blonde hair was pulled into two ponytails tied with blue ribbons. She wore the same blue-and-white checked dress. When she saw Melinda, she smiled.

"Hi, Melinda! Come out and play."

Melinda stared at the little girl. She hardly knew what to say.

Ariana's smile wavered. "Come on, Melinda. Hurry up and get your dolls! I've got a new game."

Melinda shook her head. "Ariana, look at me. I'm not little anymore."

Ariana's lower lip thrust out in a pout. "Now you're being mean."

Melinda wanted some answers. "Do you remember Rose?" she asked.

Ariana's brows came together in a frown. "Yes. Rose got big and she got mean, too. Mean like you!"

"Who are you?" Melinda burst out. "*What* are you?"

Ariana cried out angrily. Then she whirled around and ran down the path that led into the forest.

Without thinking, Melinda took off after her. She heard Ruby calling her name, but she didn't turn back.

*I'm going to find out what really happened to my mother—no matter what!* she vowed to herself.

■ ■ ■

**A**riana was a fast runner. Melinda was still sore from her accident, so it wasn't long before she had to stop and rest. She watched as Ariana disappeared into the trees.

As soon as she caught her breath, Melinda started walking in the same direction Ariana had taken. Before long, she discovered a faint trail snaking through the trees and winding up the side of the mountain. Following the trail, Melinda came to a wide meadow and what looked like the entrance to a cave.

Then she spotted Ariana sitting on a rock. She was sobbing so loudly that she didn't hear Melinda coming.

"Ariana!" Melinda cried out.

As the girl jumped up in surprise, a

strange thing began to happen. Ariana's little-girl image seemed to fade, and another image began to emerge. Melinda was aghast as she gazed at a more frightening creature than anything she'd ever seen—or even dreamed of!

When Melinda screamed, Ariana's little-girl image instantly reemerged.

Melinda turned to run, but a man dressed as a farmer was blocking her path. "Oh, dear, you saw her, didn't you?" he said in a concerned voice.

Melinda stared at him in horror. "What is Ariana—*really*?" she cried out.

"Please, don't be afraid," he begged. "We won't hurt you. Believe me, we want no more accidents."

Melinda froze. "Like my mother?" she snarled accusingly.

The man nodded. "We didn't hurt her, I promise you. The problem was that she saw Ariana the way she really is. It frightened her."

"Ariana *kidnapped* me!" Melinda

exclaimed. "*Of course* my mother was frightened."

"Ariana didn't know any better," he said. "She's only a little child."

Melinda turned at the sound of a new voice. It was a woman dressed as a farm wife. She was trying to comfort Ariana.

"You're Ariana's mother, aren't you?" Melinda guessed.

The woman nodded. "I'd tell you my name, but you wouldn't be able to pronounce it. We don't belong in your world—but I imagine you already suspected that."

Melinda nodded.

"Please," the father begged, "give us a chance to explain who we are."

Melinda thought about it. Then she agreed. The strange couple urged her to sit with them in the warm meadow grass. Ariana curled up in her mother's arms.

"We come from a distant planet," the mother said. "We arrived here nearly one hundred of your earth years ago. We are explorers."

Melinda gasped. "But that would make you—"

"Very old in earth years," the father said with a smile. "Our ship crashed on your planet—right here in this meadow. We moved it into that cave so we could repair it without being seen."

"As you saw," the mother said, "we don't *really* look like humans. When we discovered that our appearance frightened you earth people, we changed ourselves to look like you."

"Our daughter is very young," the father added. "We age much more slowly than humans do. So although Ariana is several hundred years old in *your* years, in *our* years she's still a little girl. And she's very lonely. There's no one here to keep her company."

Melinda gazed at the little girl sitting in her mother's lap.

"We've tried to keep her away from earth people," the mother added with a sigh. "But, like most children, she doesn't understand everything we try to teach her. And sometimes she doesn't obey us."

Melinda had to smile at that. She remembered a few naughty earth children she'd had to babysit when she was younger.

"What happened to my mother?" Melinda asked.

"Ariana went out to play that day," the mother said. "When she came home, she had a baby with her—you! Ariana thought you were a toy."

"We were taking you home," the father went on, "when we met Rose on the trail. She saw us as we really are. She grabbed you from my arms and ran blindly into the forest. We were afraid of what might happen, so we followed her. She tripped and fell, hitting her head against a rock. When we got to her, it was too late. The poor thing was already dead."

"Luckily, you weren't hurt in the fall," the mother said. "After we buried your mother, we returned you to your grandmother. We feared that she'd call the police. If they investigated, we might be discovered before we could finish repairing our ship. So we did a terrible thing, I'm afraid. We let your grandmother glimpse our true image. And we threatened her about *your* safety if she talked. We are so sorry to have frightened her so badly—but we didn't know what else to do!"

"Yes, she's *still* terrified of you," Melinda said. "She thinks you stole her daughter and might steal me, too."

The father nodded sadly. "Our spaceship is repaired now," he said. "We'll be leaving soon to return to our home planet. Then our daughter—" He glanced at Ariana. "—will have some playmates of her own kind."

"I'm glad," Melinda said, and she meant it. Then she added, "Before you leave, will you show me where my mother is buried?"

Ariana's parents agreed. They seemed thankful that Melinda was no longer so upset with them.

As they walked into the forest, Melinda smiled at Ariana. She reached out to take the child's hand. "I know I'm all grown up now," Melinda said in a gentle voice. "But we were friends once, weren't we? Let's be friends again."

She was rewarded when Ariana took her hand and smiled back.

■ ■ ■

About a week later, Melinda and Ruby stood in the churchyard beside Rose's flower-covered grave. Learning the truth about her daughter had finally freed Ruby from her terrible fear. And bringing Rose *home* was a great comfort.

Suddenly, they heard a deep rumble. "Did you hear that?" Melinda asked.

"Yes," Ruby replied. "Sounds like it came from up the mountain."

They both looked up just as a flash of light streaked across the sky. They smiled. "Ariana is going home—" they said at the same time, "—*at last!*"

## After-Reading Wrap-Up

1. In your opinion, did the author come up with an interest-grabbing title for this book? Think of two alternate titles that might have been used.

2. Ruby told her granddaughter that living in the city offered more opportunities than she'd have on the mountain. Was she right? Name two or three examples of such opportunities.

3. Which character in the story made a personal sacrifice to protect another? Identify that character and explain why she made that difficult choice.

4. Ruby says that "some people mature faster than others." Have you known people of the same age who are at very different stages of maturity? Describe their differences.

5. Which character in the story did you like best? Which character did you like least? Explain your reasons.

6. Science-fiction authors have written many very different descriptions of visitors from outer space. Put your own imagination to work and write a detailed description of your own invention.